For Isaac — A. McQ.
For Elliot, from Mummy, with love — R. H.

First published in the UK in 2018 by
Alanna Books
46 Chalvey Road East,
Slough, Berkshire, SL1 2LR

www.alannabooks.com

ISBN: 978-1-907825-200
Printed and bound in China

(card 1)

Zeki Gets a Checkup

by Anna McQuinn

Illustrated by Ruth Hearson

ALANNA BOOKS

Zeki is a big boy now.

Today he is going for a checkup.

Now he is big,
Zeki drinks from
his cup...

...and eats
by himself.

He loves hiding toys

and playing ball.

He loves singing

and dancing.

Wow, Zeki!

Now it is time to go. Zeki puts his toys away. Good job Zeki!

Daddy packs a bag. Zeki gets his blankie and Mister Seahorse.

At the clinic they wait their turn.

Zeki sits nicely and plays with Mister Seahorse.

It is Zeki's turn. Welcome Zeki!

Zeki shows what he can do now.

Then they check his height

and weight...

...his eyes

and ears.

Thump! Thump!
Zeki's heart sounds
great!

Then Zeki gets a jab –
it will keep him healthy.

Well done, Zeki!

Zeki gets a sticker AND a new book to read at home.

The checkup is done.
See you next time, Zeki!

More about the Lulu & Zeki books

This belongs on the shelf with the holy books. Lulu is the cutest little girl in the whole world and this book celebrates the love of libraries and learning and books and stories. This book made me so happy I cried.

Lulu loves the Library
Celebrating 10 years of Lulu!
Anna McQuinn
Rosalind Beardshaw

Anna McQuinn continues to capture the gentle, everyday moments of childhood.

The Lulu books belong in every library, nursery and children's centre. They are wonderfully inclusive and celebrate the joy of books and play.

Hearson's cheery and warm illustrations are stunning.

Zeki Loves Baby Club
by Anna McQuinn
Illustrations by Ruth Hearson

What a helpful book for parents of very young children to support their early years activities at home.

An authentic, warm and positive reflection of toddler life, let's find ways to get this book into every care setting, library, and health visitor's clinic!

Lulu Loves Stories
Anna McQuinn
Rosalind Beardshaw

Beardshaw's illustrations are full of small details that add to the warm feel.

Anna McQuinn's stories of Lulu are authentic, and totally in tune with young children's lives - the interior as well as the external.

This book is everything good.

Alanna Books has a number of titles that are beautifully delivered, with a real understanding of children and parents. They are just the sort of publisher we love! A story for everyone, about all the things that babies find good fun as they develop and increase understanding. The book is full of information for parents too.

Lulu reads to Zeki
Anna McQuinn & Rosalind Beardshaw

Rosalind Beardshaw's illustrations with their remarkable vitality, make ever more strongly and still more effectively Anna McQuinn's important message about the proper place of reading and books in children's and their families' lives.

McQuinn has a real talent for creating stories that deal with childhood's important rights of passage and pitching them perfectly for the audiences.

The roots of reading, along with matters of love and life, are happily married in this bright, uplifting, outstanding and important offering.

Zeki Can Swim!
Anna McQuinn
Illustrated by Ruth Hearson

Lulu Loves Flowers
Anna McQuinn
Illustrated by Rosalind Beardshaw

...perfect in every way. That's all you really need to know.

In the best picture book tradition, all Lulu's adventures are domestic ones centred around family, home and the local community, because we all know how exciting these everyday experiences can be.

Once again, the lovely illustrations convey the tenderness and physicality of the parent-child bond.

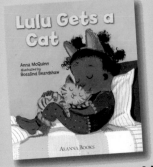
Lulu Gets a Cat
Anna McQuinn
Illustrated by Rosalind Beardshaw
ALANNA BOOKS

So. Stinking. Adorable.
Perfect for cat lovers of all ages. ★★★★★

Lulu never fails to delight: this new story ticks all the boxes for showing the very young that becoming a pet owner involves considerable responsibility, as well as introducing the basics of adopting a cat.

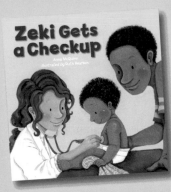
Zeki Gets a Checkup
Anna McQuinn
Illustrated by Ruth Hearson

All are joyous, full of smiles, reflecting everyday experiences of young children and highlighting things that really matter - not only but especially - with little ones: spending time together, reading and sharing stories. If you've live or work with kids under 5, I think they should form an essential part of your library.